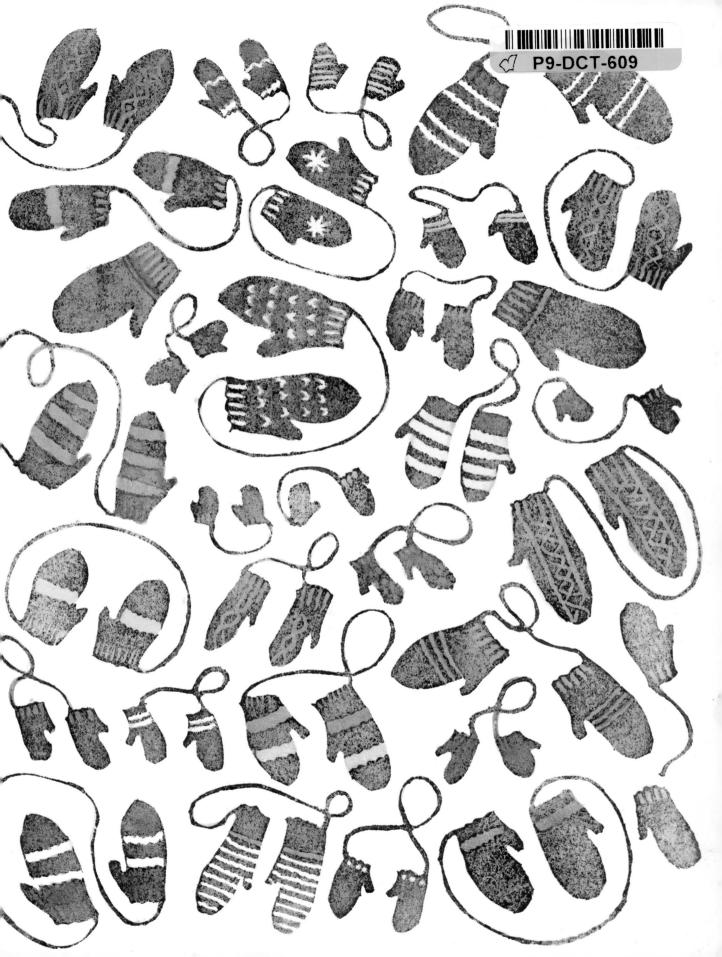

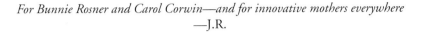

For Bunnie Rosner and Carol Corwin—and for innovative mothers everywhere
—J.R.

For Sara and Sam
—K.S.

Visit us on the Web!
randomhouse.com/kids

Educators and librarians, for a variety of teaching tools, visit us at RHTeachersLibrarians.com

Library of Congress Cataloging-in-Publication Data
Rosner, Jennifer.
The mitten string / by Jennifer Rosner ; illustrated by Kristina Swarner. — First edition.
pages   cm.
Summary: Ruthie Tober's family is known for the beautiful, warm mittens they knit so when she and her mother meet a deaf woman and her baby
and give them shelter, Ruthie decides to design very special mittens for them.
ISBN 978-0-385-37118-6 (trade) — ISBN 978-0-375-97186-0 (lib. bdg.) — ISBN 978-0-375-98173-9 (ebook)
[1. Mittens—Fiction. 2. Deaf—Fiction. 3. People with disabilities—Fiction. 4. Jews—Fiction.] I. Swarner, Kristina, illustrator. II. Title.
PZ7.R719548Mit 2014 [E]—dc23 2013018685

MANUFACTURED IN CHINA
10 9 8 7 6 5 4 3 2 1
First Edition

The Mitten String

By Jennifer Rosner

Illustrated by Kristina Swarner

RANDOM HOUSE · NEW YORK

It was said that Ruthie Tober's family warmed the hands of the entire village, because everyone who lived there, big and small, wore mittens knitted from Tober wool.

The Tobers' sheep had the fluffiest wool in the region.
On shearing days, friends and neighbors came to help
Ruthie's family clip and gather the soft, downy fleece.

The Tobers worked hard, scouring, picking, and carding the wool. Ruthie, who loved bright colors, prepared the pots for dyeing. When it was time for spinning, Ruthie's mother stood at the great wheel and spun the wool into yarn.

Most nights, Ruthie and her mother sat together and knitted. Ruthie loved how their stitches—each one a tiny knot of yarn—added up to form warm, cozy garments.

Ruthie especially enjoyed making mittens. She knitted plenty of extras in the smallest sizes, because she had noticed that many children lost mittens every winter.

Ruthie herself had lost some, her mother reminded her with a wink.

On market days, Ruthie's parents loaded their wagon with bolts of cloth and heaping baskets of yarn to sell and trade. Ruthie took along a basket of her most colorful mittens.

One day, on the way home from market, Ruthie's family came upon a woman standing with her baby at the side of the road. The woman did not speak to them. Instead, she held up a slate with a neatly printed message. Her husband had gone for help.

The Tobers invited the woman and her child to spend the night. Smiling gratefully, the woman wrote her name, BAYLA, and her baby's name, AARON, on the slate.

Ruthie noticed a length of yarn wrapped around Bayla's wrist. The yarn was the deepest blue Ruthie had ever seen—deeper even than the special blue thread braided into the white tassels of her father's prayer shawl. Ruthie imagined the mittens she could make with yarn like that!

"Why doesn't Bayla speak?" Ruthie asked her mother.

"Bayla is deaf," her mother explained. "She cannot hear, so she cannot speak. Luckily, she reads and writes. It is very wise of her to carry chalk and a slate."

Ruthie watched in amazement as Bayla communicated with Aaron using hand signs. To Ruthie, it looked as if Bayla were standing before an invisible spinning wheel, her words flowing from her fingers like delicate strands of yarn.

That night, Ruthie could not fall asleep. She
wondered what it was like for Bayla, not hearing
and not speaking. Was the silence peaceful? Or was
it lonely? If Aaron needed her during the night, how
would Bayla know?

Ruthie peered into their room. Bayla lay sleeping, one arm dangling over the side of the bed. The blue yarn was still looped around her wrist. From there, it trailed across the floor to the cradle, ending in a bow around Aaron's tiny arm!

Ruthie remembered seeing a string trail through the village
from little Sarah Lowy's sickbed to the synagogue's holy ark.
Ruthie's mother had explained that the string carried the
family's prayers for Sarah to get well again.

But why would Bayla tie a piece of yarn between herself
and her baby in the night?

Just then, Aaron began to cry. As his arms moved,
the yarn tugged Bayla awake. Bayla lifted Aaron
in a soothing embrace and warmed his chilly
hands on her cheeks.

Early the next morning, Ruthie set to work, knitting with her softest, fluffiest skein of yarn. She stitched a slender cuff and thumb, then shaped a tiny mitten top. Soon, Ruthie had one mitten, just the right size for Aaron.

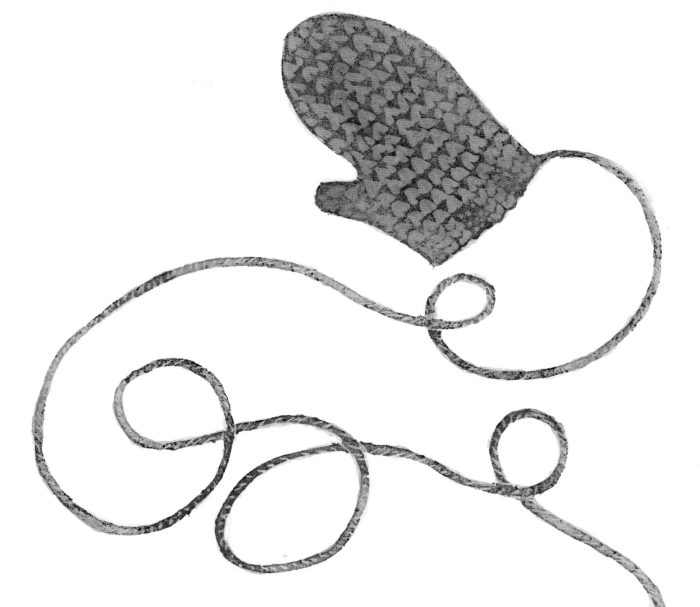

As she was about to start on the other, Ruthie had an idea!
This time, she knitted a mitten big enough to fit Bayla. Then
she connected the mittens, large and small, with a length of
string—perfect for Bayla and Aaron on the coldest nights.

When Ruthie gave her the mittens, Bayla smiled with delight. She showed Ruthie the sign for "mittens," sliding her left hand over her right and her right hand over her left. After breakfast, Ruthie knitted Bayla and Aaron each a second mitten.

Ruthie excitedly paired off the mittens for market, connecting them with a string that could be threaded through a child's coat sleeves. The string would keep the mittens from getting lost!

"You are both clever *and* kind," Ruthie's mother said, beaming with pride. "You make our world a bit better with every stitch."

Later, Bayla showed Ruthie the woody plants she could use to make a bright blue color for her dye pots. Not long after, Bayla's husband arrived with the repaired wagon, ready to take his family home for the Sabbath.

Bayla unraveled the blue yarn from her wrist and handed it to Ruthie. Ruthie wrote her thank-you on Bayla's slate. She also wrote the day of their next shearing.

By that time, Ruthie thought, Aaron would have outgrown his tiny mittens. She would make him a bigger pair—bright blue and, of course, tied together with a length of Tober yarn. Ruthie could hardly wait!

Knitting Glossary

Carding: Separating and straightening wool fibers in preparation for spinning.
Scouring: Washing wool in hot water to remove dirt and grease.
Shearing: Removing the woolen fleece of a sheep by cutting or clipping.
Skein: A wound ball of yarn with a center strand that can be pulled out.
Spinning: Twisting together wool fibers to create yarn.

Sign Language Glossary

Knit  **Wool**

Mitten*  **Yarn**

Sheep

*Users of sign language actually prefer gloves to mittens, as they employ their fingers to spell words and to sign.

Author's Note

This story honors my great-great-aunt Bayla Wertheim, who was deaf and lived in an Austrian village in the 1800s. Bayla wanted to ensure that she would wake when her baby cried in the night, so at bedtime she tied a string from her wrist to her baby's.

Acknowledgments

My deepest thanks to Naomi Kleinberg, Chris Barash, Diane Troderman, Naomi Shulman, Judith Inglese, Diana Larkin, Nancy Malina, Amy Meltzer, Catherine Newman, Michele Wick, and always, Bill Corwin and our daughters, Sophia and Juliet.

—J.R.

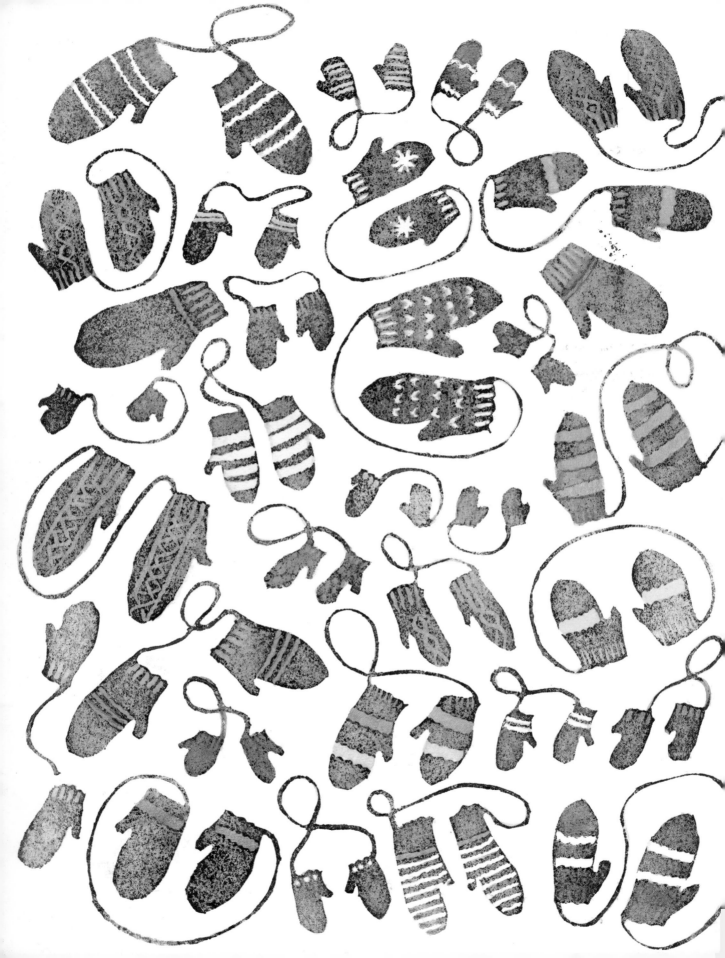